For Louis

Published in the United States 2002 by Handprint Books
413 Sixth Avenue, Brooklyn, New York 11215
www.handprintbooks.com

First American Edition
Originally published in Great Britain by Little Tiger Press
Printed in Belgium
ISBN: 1-929766-41-6
2 4 6 8 10 9 7 5 3 1

Astronaut
PiggyWiggy

Christyan and Diane Fox
Handprint Books ✋ Brooklyn, New York

Whenever I lie in bed at night, I look at the stars above and dream of what it would be like to be a daring astronaut!

I would climb into my rocket dressed in my special space suit  and prepare for launch.

I would need
lots of training
to learn how
to use all
the controls.
Then . . .

Blast off into outer space!

In space
everything floats . . .

so it would be very difficult to eat and drink!

I would have to go outside the spaceship....

to make repairs.

We would land on
exciting, faraway
planets...

and make new friends.

But I hope
there would
be time to
do all these
things . . .